BLACKBIRD

Lauren Morris

CONTENTS

WHY YOU Wanna FLY?

"Rena" a voice said jolting me from my sleep. Groaning, I turned over to see my little sister Tara with a panic-stricken look in her eyes.

"Rena, mommy's home" and instantly my body was on high alert.

"Go hide baby" I whispered. I quietly ushered her into the closet and closed the door ever so softly. The last time my mother, Teresa, came home under the influence and saw Tara she decided she looked too much like her father and burned her with a cigarette. I stood at the doorway to be sure if she was here and sure enough I heard my name being called. I put on a stoic face, preparing for the worst.

"Yes mama" I answered. She sat on the couch with hooded eyes and to the left of her was an unfamiliar man.

"Come sit next to me baby" Teresa smiled, patting the torn sofa cushion in between her and the stranger. Hesitantly I walked over to them attempting to buy myself some time. By the looks on each of their faces I could see how impatient they were becoming. When I was officially within arms reach my mother dug her nails in my arm and yanked me down next to her. "Where's the smaller one?" the man asked, clearly referring to Tara.

"She's spending the night over a friend's house" I lied through my teeth. Teresa looked at me suspiciously then at the door to our room but before she could speak he said "Don't matter, you'll do just fine"

Everything that occurred next happened so slow but also so fast at the same time. At some point my mother disappeared and no matter how much I begged him not to. No matter how much I fought, he overpowered me and I ended up underneath him just praying for it to be over.

It was as if my brain detached from the rest of my body, almost like I couldn't feel him violate me. Though I felt it all, my mind was elsewhere, I wasn't trapped under some stranger my mom pawned me off to get her daily fix. I wasn't crying silently as the pain became too much to bear. I was flying high in the clouds, like the most beautiful bird you could ever imagine.

After it was over he got up to get dressed and I ran into the bathroom locking the door behind me. I turned on the shower making the water scalding hot. I didn't care if it burned I needed to scrub the trace of him off of me; it was sickening. No matter how hard I scrub I still feel him there, inside of me, ruining me. I sat in the tub staring at the wall wanting to cry but all that came out were silent screams. I flinched at my reflection in the in the water, and all I could think was, why cant't I fly? I walked towards Tara and I's shared room but before I could open the door the stranger smacked my ass and grabbed my arm forcefully.

"That was fun, make sure you bring your little sister next time" he winked. I nodded fearfully in agreement hoping he'd let me go and after looking longingly at my body one last time he released me and walked away. I entered the room and put a chair under the doorknob, making it hard for any unwanted person to come in.

"You can come out now Tara" I whispered. She emerged from the closet and sat on the bed next to me.

"Rena, I'm hungry" she whined.

"I know but I'll get us up super early tomorrow so you can get to breakfast on time at school, deal?" I asked.

"Deal" she agreed happily. I eventually coaxed her to sleep and laid beside her, stroking her hair. She deserves the world, more than what her 17 year old sister and druggy mother can give her. I stared at the ceiling, getting lost in my own thoughts, knowing that sleep wouldn't find me tonight.

I kept my promise and got her to school on time, as for me I was going to be late 1st period again. The halls were empty when I finally made it to school. I could just skip, but my only other option was home with Teresa. I sighed and opened the door to the first class of the day. I hoped they wouldn't stare and that Mr. Vincent wouldn't question me, but that's what I get for hoping. All eyes were on me as soon as I walked in.

"Miss Klein, where have you been" he questioned me as I made my way to my seat. I could hear snickers all over the classroom.

"Looks like she's been rummaging through someone's garbage can" Kathy giggled making the whole class erupt in laughter, I even saw Mr. Vincent bite back a chuckle. I just sat stone faced staring ahead at the chalkboard.This is how majority of my classes go, me as the butt of everyone's joke. After the class settled down we began our work, I was doing just fine until I noticed wrappers and crumpled up paper being thrown in my direction. A couple bounced off my head, hitting their target I clenched my pencil in frustration but I knew what would happened if I got in trouble. For me that would mean extra time at home with the mother of the year. I breathed a sigh of relief at the sound of the school bell grateful to be done with this class but dreading the repetition the was to come. I kept my head down as I walked the halls careful to avoid bumping into anyone.

At lunch I sat alone and ate quietly, I was just grateful I made it to my only meal of the day. I didn't bother anyone and I didn't want anyone to bother me. To everyone else here l was the loner, weird girl who wore dirty, baggy clothes. I sat in silence and basked in my time of not being humiliated by my peers. My moment of solace didn't last long as everyone started the transition to our next class. I entered the Biology lab and sat in my usual seat in the back. The rest of the class shuffled in and Ms. Night went to the front of the class.

"Alright you guys settle down" Ms. Night said. " As you all may know It's almost time for midterms but before we get into that half of you are currently failing my class and if you don't manage to get your grades up, you won't even have to worry about the midterm because you'll be taking my class again" she stated. There were groans all over the class coming from those who know they slacked off. I just turned my attention to window to watch the birds in the courtyard. Personally, I didn't care I had more important things to worry about than cellular respiration.

"If I call out your name come see me before the end of class for extra credit" Ms. Night called out. She read off a list of names and of course mine was included but as the class came to an end I found myself walking right past her desk.

BLACKBIRD.

I stood outside until the locker room was empty to change back into my regular clothes after gym class. After I was sure everyone was gone I went inside, picked a corner and began to undress. I had gotten my shirt back on but my bottom half was uncovered when I heard voices approaching. My heart was racing and beating so loudly I could hear it in my ears.

"I think I left my makeup bag in here" Katherine's distinctive voice resonated of the lockers. Kathy Unlander, the worst of them all, I tensed up at the sound of her voice. "Well look who we have here" she smirked, her eyes falling on me. As if on cue a posse of girls filed in, surrounding me.

"If it isn't scrawny legged Blackbird" Kathy snickered. I finally managed to get my pants on, attempting to ignore them. I gathered my things heading for the exit when Naomi blocked my way.

"Where you flying off to Blackbird" she smirked pushing me backwards. I pushed her back and she hauled off and punched me in the stomach. I groaned and leaned over, crumpling to the ground. She bent down, whispering in my ear menacingly "Careful little girl, or you'll get your wings snipped" I just closed my eyes and waited until their footsteps retreated. When they were gone I slowly pulled myself up off the floor wiping my stray tears. I'm not sure how much time had passed but the campus was nearly empty by the time by the time I exited the building.

"Hey you need a ride" a voice called out. I looked up it was one of my classmates, Evan Parker. I stopped and looked him dead in the eye then a continued walking. I stopped at Tara's school to pick her up and she was waiting at the steps with her teacher. Her face instantly lit up when she saw me, making me smile.

"Ready to go babycakes" I asked, offering my hand. She nodded and laced her fingers through mine and we walked home while she told me every detail of her day. When we arrived at our house I was thankful to discover that Teresa wasn't there but surprisingly there was food.

"Where's mommy?" Tara asked.

"She's running some errands she'll be back" I replied. Truthfully I had no clue where she was but what's new. I made us a quick dinner then took it to our room where Tara was doing homework. I handed her a plate then we sat on the bed and began to eat.

"I like it when we have food" she said giddily taking bites out of her spaghetti.

"Me too" I agreed.

I gave Tara her bath and put her to bed then I took a shower right after. As I lie down, I thought about how each day just seems to get harder. My will is seemingly withering away, but I have a responsibility to keep going, for Tara. If I give up, then she has no one. I dozed off, I woke to Teresa gently shaking me. I jumped up, shielding Tara behind me.

"Get up you two it's time for school" she smiled. Just when I thought it couldn't get any worse we were back at Phase Two. Phase Two when my mother seems to just get better overnight then a stressful situation will occur and it's back to Phase One. I got Tara and I dressed and ready to go and my mother had breakfast waiting for us.

"What's this" I asked hesitantly.

"Breakfast, I know you guys are late so just take it with you, I'll see you later" she kissed Tara's cheek and tried the same with me but I jerked away from her. We ate our breakfast along the way, and as usual I dropped Tara off and made my way to school. All of this was nice and all but deep down I knew, something isn't right.

I forced myself through my everyday ritual of being picked on and harassed by everyone. I'm so used to it that it doesn't usually bother me but today, my anxiety has had me worked up about my mother, about what was to come. I was so into my thoughts I was startled when Ms. Night called on me.

"Rena, could you come up here please" I noticed Evan standing by her desk. I slowly slid out of my seat and shuffled to the front of the classroom.

"So from my observation you and Mr. Parker here are the only two who have not inquired about extra credit. Will you tell me why that is?" she questioned, I kept my eyes on my shoes and just shrugged.

"I see" she pursed her lips and sighed "Well I'm not sure if you two are aware but I'm the cliche hardass teacher that doesn't want to see my students fail, especially if I see the potential they possess. So I'm assigning you two to do a group project, it will be due in 4 weeks. I want you to create a detailed presentation about the phases of mitosis with a diorama included" she smiled brightly, not really giving us an option. I nodded and quickly returned to my seat, Evan didn't look too happy but neither was I. Internally I cursed Ms. Night for giving me more stress than I needed but I slowly found myself smiling at the realization that she thought I had potential.

YOU AIN'T EVER GONNA FLY

"Hey, wait up" a voice called, I ignored it and kept walking. Someone then grabbed my shoulder and I spun around angrily. "Woah, easy tiger I just want to talk about the project" Evan said holding his hands up in surrender.

"Oh, sorry" I mumbled.

"Are you free this afternoon we could start on it, if you want" he suggested.

"My sister...I have to pick her up from school" I replied finding an excuse to avoid the meeting. I started walking again and he stepped in front of me, blocking my path.

"I have a car we can pick her up, she can come along too if you'd like" he smiled. I opened my mouth to protest but his face said he wasn't taking no for an answer.

"Ok, we can only stay for a little while" said quietly

"That's cool, my car is this away" he led me down the hall and I followed a few feet behind. I didn't want to embarrass him by making people think we were together. His car was the closest parked to the entrance door in the the parking lot. He unlocked the car doors to his Range Rover and we climbed in " Your sister, she goes to the elementary school a few blocks from here right?"

"Yeah how'd you know" I questioned suspiciously.

"I see you guys walking to school sometimes, I think I drive the same route you walk. I offered you a ride one time but I get it stranger danger" he chuckled. After a short drive we pulled in front of her school. Tara was sitting on the steps with her teacher waiting for me. I got out my heart lighting up at the sight of my cheerful little sister.

"Hey babygirl, we're going to go by a friends house today. You ready?" I asked.

"Okay, bye Ms. Maddock" she said turned to her teacher waving her goodbye. I opened the backdoor, she climbed inside and I buckled her seatbelt. I got back in the car and prepared for the drive to Evan's house.

"Hi, I'm your sister's friend Evan what's your name" he asked focused on the road but seemingly interested in interacting with Tara.

"Tara, you said you're my sissy's friend, that's so good...I didn't think she had any" she replied, I mentally face palmed.

"Tara, that's a pretty name and of course we go way back" he smiled. We pulled into the driveway of a really nice house well pretty much anything is really nice compared to where we live. We walked onto the porch and he unlocked the front door for us to go inside.

"Evan" a little boy screamed running up to him.

"Hey kiddo" he replied ruffling his hair "This is my brother Ethan"

"Rena, I'm thirsty" Tara whined tugging on my sleeve.

"We have snacks c'mon" Ethan said grabbing her hand.

"Wa-wait don't-"

"It's okay, my mom won't mind" he reassured me. Still I followed behind Tara just to keep an eye on her. I ended up following them into a kitchen where a dark haired woman stood at the stove handing Tara and Ethan juice box and sandwiches. When she looked up at me she smiled the brightest smile I had ever seen.

"Hi I'm Evan's mom Vanessa, you must be Rena" she chirped.

"Yes ma'am, I'm sorry about my sister-"

"It's no trouble, we have plenty to go around" Vanessa assured me.

"Told ya" Evan chuckled "You ready to start on the project?"

"Yeah, can we sit in here. I don't like to let her out of my sight for long" I mumbled sheepishly.

"Sure, that's cool just let me go get my laptop" Evan said. While I waited his mom slid a sandwich in front of me and I wanted to protest but my stomach growled in disagreement.

"Thank you, for being so nice" I said gratefully

"It's no problem sweetie, are people usually not not nice?" she asked, I looked down at my hands and thankfully Evan walked back in with his laptop cutting her off. I could tell she wanted to say something else but instead she went back to cleaning, not wanting to intrude. After a few hours of doing research and taking notes Evan offered to take us home."So this is where you live?" Evan asked parked in front of our visibly old house.

"Yeah, um see you tomorrow. Let's go Tara" I said getting out the car.

"Bye Evan" she said cheerily, he just smiled and waved back at her. We walked inside and there was new furniture and decorations, it made the house look almost decent. I kept Tara close to my side waiting for Teresa to make an entrance but she never showed.

"Hey Rena" a male voice said making me instantly sick to my stomach. No, she wouldn't let my rapist back in here but the more I thought the more I knew that she would have in fact let him come back.

"Tara, go to the room don't come out unless I say so" I said. She ran towards the room and he grabbed her tiny arm. "Don't you fucking touch her" I screamed jumping on his back and started hitting him with everything in me which made him let her go get me off of him.

"You little bitch" he growled tossing me onto the ground.

"Run Tara" I yelled. He snatched me up by my hair then wrapped his hands around my throat. My vision started to go black as I slowly lost oxygen then he dropped me to the floor. I started to crawl away, hoping he was finished. He then kicked me in my ribs afterwards he began to forcefully tug off my clothes, so much for flying right? All I could think was at least his attention was off of Tara for the time being. Teresa came in just as he was finishing up. She looked at me in horror.....maybe she had changed.

"I told you not to be so rough this time Vick, look at the bruises. You okay baby?" she asked hugging me, I shoved her away from me in disgust.

"There's the money Theresa, see you next time Rena" he winked at me and pulled up his pants and walked out the front door.

"Look Rena, I know this is hard but we need this money. You're doing a good thing for your sister and I" she said sympathetically.

"You're such a sorry excuse for a mother" I spat. I went in the bathroom to assess the damage and Teresa was right he left bruises that were going to be impossible to cover up. What's the point of praying, no one is going to come save us.

NO PLACE BIG ENOUGH FOR HOLDING

I sat upright at the sound of an alarm going off in Tara and I's newly furnished room. Making a sudden movement getting out of bed caused me to wince in pain. My inner thighs, arms, and neck felt sore, I pushed through it, to get Tara dressed. My mother is pimping me out to provide for us, it hurts to even admit it in my head. I wish it weren't true, I wish that Tara could have the mother she deserves but all she has is me. When I finished getting myself together we made our way to the kitchen. Of course Teresa was there, cooking without a care in the world, as if she didn't condone of the rape of her daughter multiple times but this isn't anything new.

"Breakfast my lovelies I-" Teresa said cheerily, I looked at her with so much hatred in my eyes. You know that saying, 'if looks could kill', then she'd be a dead woman.

"Grab something to eat so we can go" I instructed Tara, she nodded and grabbed some pop tarts and bottle of apple juice.

"Look Rena-"

"Save it Teresa, let's go Tara" she took my hand and we walked out the door ignoring every advance from my mother. Every step I took throbbed, I wish she would have at least got some pain killers for the house, this walk was going to be horrible. By the time we made it to Tara's school I was in so much pain. I smiled and waved until I watched her go inside then I sat on the steps to take a break. A few seconds passed and suddenly a car horn honked and I looked up to see Evan.

"Hey are you okay, I saw you limping and I figured you could use the ride" he offered.

"I'm fine, thanks" I stood too quickly causing me to grimace, and I'm sure he noticed.

"Just get in we're going to the same place" he said, groaning internally I weighed the options in my head. If I don't take the ride I'll be late, so I might as well. I limped to the car and slowly took my time getting in careful not to make any more sudden movements. Evan watched with so much curiosity I knew questions were to come. Sure enough a few minutes passed and he broke the silence.

"Why are you limping, you get into a fight or something?" he asked. I stayed quiet, avoiding his concerned gaze. "Was it one the kids from school?"

"No" I replied, he noticed my look of annoyance and he held his hand up in surrender.

"I'll chill, it's none of my business anyway" he stated but I saw him look over at me once more but he didn't continue. I sighed in relief as the school came to view and we pulled into the parking lot.

"Thanks...for the ride" I blurted out and before he could say anything I limped away. When I made it inside I rushed to restroom and collapsed inside a stall. I sat on the floor waiting for the pain to stop. Millions of thoughts racked my brain; why can't I have a normal life, what did I do to deserve this, when will I ever catch a break? I didn't realize I was crying until I felt the tears roll down my face. I wiped my tears off on the back of my sleeve and unlocked the stall door to get water from the sink.

"Whoa, is that little miss Blackbird" a voice said. I dried my face and it was Kathy, smirking at me and I braced myself for what was to come.

"What do you want?" I questioned.

"Feisty today are we Blackbird, but weren't you just in there crying" she laughed. I rolled my eyes, gathering my things hoping she'd take the hint and leave. Kathy into my path and crossed her arms not letting me by. I prayed to God that she wouldn't hit me, haven't I been beaten up enough?

"Move." I mumbled, she jumped at me causing me to flinch. Making her laugh very loudly, then she stepped to the side. I took that as my ticket to escape, and surprisingly she let me go.

"There's no place to hide from me Blackbird, I'll see you around" she called after me. I didn't even look back, my fast paced walk became a jog and I turned the corner and bumped into Evan.

"Hey, I was looking for you" he stated.

"Why" I snapped

"Calm down, I just wanted to check on you. Have you been crying?" he questioned

"Wh-what, no I have to get to class" I stammered and limped past him, I could still feel him staring at me as a walked away from him. I never thought there would be a day that I was glad I made it to class. At lunch I was sitting by myself at my usual table when I was interrupted by Evan with his lunch tray.

"Hey" he smiled

"Sup" I replied quietly

"You mind if I sit here?" he asked gesturing towards the empty seat in front of me. I shrugged, and he took it as an invitation anyway and sat down. "Why aren't you eating" he looked at my still full tray of school food.

"Not hungry" I stated.

"You should probably eat something you look sick" he commented, then he slapped his hand over his mouth.

"Thanks, that's a step up from the things I've been called before" I laughed humorlessly

"No I didn't mean it like that, I can tell by your face that you haven't eaten and that's not good, but I'm not saying you're not pretty, you're cute like a puppy. Not saying you remind me of a dog...and I'm gonna shut up now" he rambled. I laughed at his antics internally, causing me to smirk, I hope he didn't think I took offense. "I got a smile, I knew my awkwardness would pay off someday" he laughed. At the end of the day I met Evan at his car so we could work on the project.

"We getting your little sister today?" he asked.

"Everyday...we have to get her everyday" I said. He nodded and a few minutes later we arrived at the school to pick her up. When we pulled up her teacher, Ms. Maddock, was waiting on the curb with her as usual. I got out to open the door for Tara and as she got in her teacher pulled me aside.

"Rena, is everything okay at home?" she asked with a look of concern.

"Yes ma'am, everything is good why?"

"Tara told me some disturbing news today. She broke down in class crying and when I asked why she said that a bad man has been coming by at night and hurting you." she stated. My eyes started to well up and my legs got weak.

"I ha-have no idea what you're ta-talking about" I stuttered.

"Rena if something is happening you need to tell someone Tara is afraid but I think it's more for you than herself" she said.

"We have to go" I snatched my arm out of her grip, and sped walk back to the car. "Drive." I instructed and he did just that, I watched in the rear-view mirror as we left Ms. Maddock in the dust.

"What was all that about, the conversation looked pretty serious" Evan asked.

"Nothing important, don't worry about it" I mumbled.

ALL THE TEARS YOU'RE GONNA CRY

We walked inside Evan's house and before Tara could run off I pulled her to the side. I waited until everyone else was out of ear shot then I spoke. "What happened at school today?"

"Please don't be mad" she began to cry " I just wanted to help, I don't want you to die" I grabbed her little hands and kissed her forehead.\

"Shh baby, its okay I'm not mad. We just can't tell anyone or they'll separate us, don't you worry okay things will get better" I reassured her.

"But if you die, who will be my mommy then" she sobbed, making my heart ache.

"Nothing bad is going to happen to me Tara, and no matter what I will always be your mommy, and I will always be there to protect you okay?" she sniffled and nodded, I hugged her once more then wiped her tears.

"I love you with all my heart kid" I said causing her to smile again.

"I love you too" she smiled and in that moment it felt worth it. Like the abuse didn't matter as much, as long as I could keep a smile on her face, as long as she was safe everything would be okay. I wiped her face off and she ran off to find Ethan so they could play. I couldn't ignore the horrible pain shooting through my body any time I moved. Everything hurt and I felt so dizzy, I leaned against the wall to support myself.

"Rena, everything okay" Evan questioned.

"Yeah, I'm fine" I nodded.

"C'mon you need something to eat" he put my arm around his shoulder and slowly helped me walk to the kitchen. Ms. Vanessa dropped the tupperware she was holding when she saw me.

"Oh my god, Rena are you okay" Vanessa asked coming to my aid.

"I'm-"

"She hasn't been eating, I'll fix her something" Evan said then turned to me "can you make it to the chair by yourself"

I nodded in reply, and took one step causing the pain to intensify. I tried not to grimace as I took the next step, my legs then buckled under pressure and suddenly I was collapsing making everything go dark. I woke up to the sound of a monitor beeping and the smell of antiseptic. I opened my eyes and observed the room it was all white with a couple of black chairs which were occupied by Evan and Ms. Vanessa. After a few moments they noticed that I was awake and Ms. Vanessa said something to Evan then she left the room.

"How are you feeling?" Evan asked approaching the hospital bed.

"Tired " I answered. Before he could say anything else Ms. Vanessa returned with a dark haired, brown skinned woman wearing a doctor's coat.

"Hi Rena, I'm Dr. Fatima. I have a few questions for you okay sweetie?" she said, I nodded slowly. "Have you ever been a victim of abuse?" my eyes widened, and I looked at her then at Evan and Ms. Vanessa who didn't seem to think the question was preposterous.

"Wh-what, no" I replied nervously.

"Rena if you're scared it's okay we have people here who can help you" Dr. Fatima stated.

"I have no idea what you're talking about" I said defensively.

"Rena you have two cracked ribs, bruises all over your body, and you're very malnourished. You also have a severe amount of internal damage to your vagina" she blatantly stated. I couldn't even speak, what could I say? I just burst out into tears, and Ms. Vanessa attempted to console me. I felt hysterical, I was wailing and sobbing and Evan watched. He looked like he hated seeing me like this I could've sworn I saw a few tears fall down his face. After a few more minutes of crying I calmed down, I was ready to talk. I did a rape kit and afterwards Dr. Fatima brought a couple of police officers in so I could give them a statement.

"Since I was young my mom brought different men in, the first one though he touched me and told me not to say anything and at first I didn't but when I finally did, my mom said she didn't believe me. But now, come to think of it because he was her supplier she probably let him do it. The men came and went and after a while they lost interest in me. Until about a month ago, Vick came. H-he wanted my sister, and I couldn't let him do that to her" I was crying again, and everyone else looked completely horrified, though I continued "I thought maybe he'll never come back, until he did, we came home there was new furniture in our dingy house. And he was there, he physically went after Tara and I stopped him but then he was set on me. He beat me up and raped me. After it was over my mom showed up and she admitted that she let him do it but because he left us money and we weren't starving I was doing our family a favor." I finished.

"Ma'am, I know this maybe be strange but you are the bravest girl I've ever met in my day." one of the cops said solemnly, I gave him a half-hearted smile and him an his partner left the room.

"Where's Tara?" I asked.

"She's at my house with Ethan and the babysitter" Ms. Vanessa reassured me. I sighed and relaxed into my pillow noticing Evan's face and I beckoned him over to me. I grabbed his hand and gave the biggest smile I could muster.

"It's okay, we're gonna be okay thanks to you" I said.

"H-how could someone do something so disgusting? How" he asked angrily, he had tears running down his face that I'm not sure he was even aware of.

"I don't know, I've wondered that too" I replied.

"You need to rest okay, we're gonna go check on the kids and we'll be back" Ms. Vanessa said patting my arm.

"I'll stay, to keep an eye on her" Evan said and pulled up a chair next to the bed. She nodded and exited the room. "Try to get some rest" he said to me, I closed my eyes and drifted off to sleep and for the first time in a long time, I felt safe.

I woke up to the sound of angry whispers. I could see Evan on the phone, pacing the room. Then I heard him say "What do you mean their mom came to get Tara?"

I sat straight up in bed, startling Evan. He noticed the look on my face, I ripped the iv out of my arm and proceeded to get up.

"Rena" he yelled.

"I have to go" I said getting out of the bed. He grabbed me trying to restrain me as carefully as possible. The nurses must have heard us because they ran into the room.

"Calm down, Miss" one of them said.

"No, let me go, please they're gonna hurt her" I screamed. Then I felt a needle in my arm and my vision started to blur, I could feel my grip loosening. "P-please don't let them hurt her" I whispered then my world went black. When I came to I was back in the hospital bed with the iv's in my arm. This time Ms. Vanessa, Ethan, and Evan were all in the room. I noticed they had all been crying, when I didn't see Tara I was instantly on high alert.

"Where is Tara" I asked hoping that maybe she was just with an officer.

"I'm so sorry, Rena" Ms. Vanessa sobbed, my mind was racing, why was she crying?

"Where is my little sister?" I asked again, only this time I was louder. They were silent for a few seconds trying to find the words to tell me.

"She's dead, he killed her" Evan replied.....You ever felt your heart shatter into a million tiny pieces and it's like the world will come crumbling down at any second? Well that doesn't even begin to describe the half of what I felt.

Your Mama's Name Was Lonely

"Rena you have to eat something" Ms. Vanessa said sliding a plate of food in front of me. I just stared at it blankly, I didn't have an appetite. How could I eat when my little sister was dead? The reason I kept going, the reason I fought so hard, the reason I felt like there was some good left in the world is dead, and she's never coming back. I was supposed to protect her from them and I failed. "Tara wouldn't want-"

"Don't say her name" I snapped. Ms. Vanessa looked surprised, it was the first words I'd spoken in days. After they told me that she died I begged them to tell me how. I cried and screamed until they did, then I wished I hadn't. She had been raped and beaten to death and they still haven't caught him but Teresa is in jail awaiting sentencing. She doesn't deserve to be called a mother, matter of fact she doesn't deserve to be alive; she is a monster. Teresa Klein wife of Daniel Klein, mother to Tara Williams and Rena Klein. Before they became tainted by drugs and alcohol they were good parents.

They loved me, but at some point they decided they loved heroin and alcohol better. I remember that they used to love reading me to sleep and taking me on long walks in the park then we'd get ice cream. We'd watch cartoons every Saturday morning after cooking breakfast together. We were a family, a real one then something changed. Teresa was a whole new person, it was like the sparkle in her eye began to fade, I was 5. My dad, Daniel, saw it too so instead of getting her help he picked up a bottle and never put it back down. I'll get to his story later but Teresa brought in waves of random men after he was gone. One of them ended up being Tara's dad but just like the rest he didn't stay long. None of them were consistent and that's probably why she was so lonely. Doesn't give her an excuse to be a piss poor excuse for a human being but she wasn't always that way.

Today I was supposed to be checking out of the hospital and taken home but instead I'm stuck here on suicide watch and they're bringing in a psychiatrist to evaluate my mental state. If you want to know how I feel, one word that begins to describe it is empty. Everyday it gets harder to keep going. Days go by and Evan comes in and climbs onto the bed next to me it's seems to be a ritual now. Being around him makes my reality seem a little less real. Sometimes he will play music and we'll sit in silence, though his presence is comforting. Other times he'll read me poetry. After weeks of listening and not hearing, one day I did. Out of his pocket he pulled his usual piece of paper with words scrawled on it and he read.

"A free bird leapson the back of the wind and floats downstream till the current endsand dips his wingin the orange sun raysand dares to claim the sky.

But a bird that stalksdown his narrow cagecan seldom see throughhis bars of ragehis wings are clipped and his feet are tiedso he opens his throat to sing.

The caged bird sings with a fearful trill of things unknown but longed for still and his tune is heard on the distant hill for the caged bird sings of freedom.

The free bird thinks of another breezeand the trade winds soft through the sighing treesand the fat worms waiting on a dawn bright lawnand he names the sky his own

But a caged bird stands on the grave of dreams his shadow shouts on a nightmare scream his wings are clipped and his feet are tied so he opens his throat to sing.

The caged bird sings with a fearful trill of things unknown but longed for still and his tune is heard on the distant hill for the caged bird sings of freedom"

"That's Maya Angelou" I spoke quietly. He nodded and handed the paper to me. I stared at the paper taking in the words. "Evan?"

"Yeah Rena?" he replied.

"I'm that caged bird"

"I know but you don't have to continue being caged......you can be free"

YOUR DADDY'S NAME WAS PAIN

I said I'd get to his story later well it's later now. Daniel Klein was once a god fearing man who loved his wife and child. He had warm eyes, a kind heart, and a cheerful smile for everyone. That's how he used to be until he noticed his wife start to drift, then he lost his way.It happened slowly at first then all at once. He noticed Teresa staying out late and he'd wait for her for hours. I'd get up in the middle of the night for water and he'd still be up waiting. I'd walk over to him to see if he was okay....he looked tired, oh so tired, but he'd just say

"I'm fine babygirl go on back to bed" he'd kiss my forehead, hand me my usual water then usher me back to my room.

Night after night it happened until he just snapped. It wasn't my need for a glass of water that brought me out of bed it was the loud commotion of him throwing things and flipping the furniture over.

Like every night I walked over to him to see if he was okay. He turned to me with a almost empty bottle of alcohol in hand with a look of disgust in his eyes.

"Go to bed" he said.

"But the furniture-" I was cut off by the feeling of being slapped in the face. He hit me so hard I fell on the ground with tears in my eyes I backed away from him.

"Didn't I tell yo ass to go to bed, you don't listen...just like ya mama" he yelled. Sobbing I picked myself up off the floor and went back to bed. After that happened I never got out of bed at night anymore. No matter how much noise he made or how many times I'd hear him hit Teresa when she finally came home, I never got up. He died from heart failure while waiting for her to come home one night. I could've saved him if I had just came out of the room to call 911 but I was too afraid. I didn't want him to get angry and hit me again.

He was dead by the time an ambulance arrived and she blamed me. She blamed a scared child for the death of her alcoholic husband. Daniel was a good man at first but that's how it always starts out. She drove my father to that bottle but he should've been strong enough to fight it. It pains me to think about what I had and what I've lost. Tara was my light but in a world full of darkness there will be something that will snuff out the light.

"Rena" Ms. Eden called. I looked from the window and back to her. She's the psychiatrist they brought in for me to talk to. "What are you thinking about Rena"

I stared at her silently before answering "Nothing" with a shrug.

"It seems to be something, you drifted off again" she stated. Don't get me wrong Ms. Eden isn't bad but I'd rather swallow glass shards than sit down and talk about my feelings with someone who couldn't even possibly relate to even a fraction of my life.

"I was thinking about how nothing will ever get better" I replied truthfully.

"Rena, we both know that's not true" she said her voice full of pity.

"Lady if you actually believe that then you haven't been listening to anything I've told you" I laughed humorlessly.

And They Call You "Little Sorrow"

There was a knock from outside of the door and I heard Evan's voice;

"Rena are you ready to go" he asked. I looked in the mirror to give myself a once-over; bags under my eyes, distressed version of a puff, chapped lips, with a dead look in my eye. I had on a black dress and flats that Ms. Vanessa bought for me. I had been dreading this day for the longest but I knew I'd have to face it at some point. Today was the day of Tara's funeral, I was going to bury my baby sister who I raised as if she was my child.

"Rena" he said again causing me to jump.

"I'm coming" I replied. I opened the door to see Even propped against the wall with a black suit on and a solemn look in his eyes, he looked nice. I could tell how uncomfortable he was in the suit by the way he kept fidgeting. I gave him a half smile signaling that I was ready, we walked out and Ms. Vanessa and Ethan were waiting for us. Tara's dad had been contacted and he made a deal that he'd pay for the funeral expenses as long as he had nothing to do with planning it. Apparently he was married and had his own little family, he didn't want his wife to know that he had stepped out on her years ago.

As the church slowly came into view my stomach dropped, I was about to see her for the last time in a casket. Saying goodbye to Tara for good was something I never thought I'd have to do. Although, I expected it to just be us but I noticed some kids from her school with their parents and some of the faculty. We got out of the car and made our way inside of the building, I could hear the organ playing some sad song. I couldn't focus on the words because as I neared the casket all I could think about was her. My knees started to get weak and Evan grabbed my waist to steady me. I looked in his eyes for a minute and it was like he gave me the little bit of strength I needed. At the front was a small baby blue casket, fit for a child, inside lay my sister.

Her brown curls were pinned up with a blue bow, with a matching blue dress and shoes. Which is fitting being that it is....well was her favorite color. I made it to her and grabbed her little hand holding it once more. I got choked on my tears at the feel of the coldness.

Her usual glowing brown skin was now pale and lifeless. The little girl in the casket was unrecognizable, she is not the Tara I know and remember. I can always recall her smiling and giggling all the time unbeknownst to the fact that we had been dealt the short hand in the card game of life. I always knew that I had to keep going for her, to survive for her, to live for her.

I stood there drowning in my tears with The Parker's by my side crying but keeping me steady. Eventually I was led to my seat which had a front row showing to my dead sister. Everyone else quietly filed in and took their seats as well. The pastor started the sermon but I could barely hear him over my cries. Evan held me the entire time, I could feel his anger and his sadness. I wanted to tell him there was nothing he could have done, nothing any of us could have done. Though the words would not come out. Finally I found the courage to look up at her again. She looked a sleeping doll, a piece of plastic all made up.

"Rena, they're waiting for you" Ms. Vanessa said. I gazed around and everyone was looking at me expectantly. I had already forgotten that I had agreed to speak. Evan gave me a small reassuring smile and I took a deep breath, before I stood. I walked behind the podium and closed my eyes remembering how Tara looked when she smiled, she had the most beautiful smile. Even with her missing baby teeth, I thought that made her look even more adorable. I opened my eyes again and Evan mouthed 'take your time'.

"Tara always had the biggest imagination. She would be a unicorn in a mystical forest, a queen of a faraway kingdom, and sometimes an astronaut in space. But to all of us, she was an amazing friend, a student, and most of all my sister. She was so young but was aware of more than I realized. Though that didn't matter she went to school every single day with a smile on her face and love in her heart. She did not deserve this, no child does.....I loved my little sister and it kills me everyday knowing that I wasn't there to protect her. Now I may not have given birth to her, but I was her mother. I held her when she cried, I stayed up watching her while she had the flu, and maybe I wasn't perfect but I did my best. I sometimes wake up hoping that this is all just a bad dream then I come to the realization that it wasn't. She had to grow up and be a trooper at such an early age because of a monster who hides behind a woman. Tara is now my little free bird who doesn't have to fight anymore, now she is flying in the sky with the angels"

Because You'll Never Love Again

I don't think I have been the same since I watched them lower Tara into the ground. Seeing something like that changes people I guess. Her dad did show up at the graveyard he stood in the back with an emotionless look on his face. Afterwards when everyone began to disband he approached me with his head hung low.

"I'm sorry for your loss, I don't think I can ever forgive myself for not doing anything sooner" he said tearfully. Before I could reply he walked away but all I could think was 'Me either dude, me either'. I was now sitting on the couch in my hospital room for my weekly session with Ms. Eden.

"Rena how are you feeling?" she asked. I slowly turned my head to look at her with a blank look on my face, then I huffed in annoyance.

"Ms. Eden how do you think, I'm feeling" I replied dully.

"I think you are in a lot of pain, you feel angry, and you feel as no one understands you" she said.

"Do you know someone else who was raped and beaten then forced to become a parent to a child she didn't create, only for that child who in the end was also raped and beaten to death. I had to bury my sister Ms. Eden, I watched them lower her body six feet into the ground. The same sister I raised and protected for as long as I could.....excuse my French but I know for a fucking fact no one understands me" I stated.

"What about Evan?" she asked

"What about him?" I countered.

"He clearly cares about you and we all see how he looks at you. You two are clearly inseparable" she stated

"He's my best friend and he feels sorry for me, of course he'd treat me like a wounded animal" I shrugged.

"Are you sure that's it? How do you feel about him?" she asked. The questions rang out in my head, and I thought about Evan really thought about him. How he read to me, held my hand, told corny jokes in an attempt to get me to smile even just a little, laid with me while I cried, and never left my side; with Evan I was never alone but deep down I am numb and I couldn't possibly feel love, not anymore.

"I feel and immense sense of gratitude towards him for never giving up on me"

"Is that all Rena?"

"That is all Ms. Eden"

"How did it make you feel about the fact that your grandmother relinquished her rights to you and let you go with Evan's family"

"I feel nothing really, she didn't want anything to do with me which isn't that surprising. I'm glad I get to go with people I trust" I shrugged, they had contacted Teresa's mother, I thought she was dead at least that's what I was always told. Though lo' and behold she was still living and breathing, and of course wanted nothing to do with me. No one wants the burden of a broken child, except Vanessa of course, that woman is a saint. She is like the mother I never had. "Are we done now? I'm ready to go home"

"Sure Rena, we can wrap it up early. Same time next week, next time at my office?" she smiled.

"Wouldn't miss it for the world" I laughed humorlessly. Ms. Eden collected her things and gave a warm smile and left the room. Shortly after Evan, Ethan and Vanessa entered with balloons and flowers.

"You ready to go home?" Evan asked smiling from ear to ear and for a moment looking at the three of them for a quick second I thought that maybe, just maybe I could try to be happy again.

SO WHY YOU wanna FLY?

I sat down on the bed in my new room, they had decorated it just for me. Nothing too fancy but it wasn't plain either. I had my own bed that wasn't on the floor or dirty and smelled like a dumpster. I had a dresser with books of poetry to read on it, there were clothes hung up in the closet and shoes under the bed. There was even a school picture of Tara on the nightstand.

"We thought you'd like the picture, if it's too much we can put it away for you" Evan said standing in the doorway.

"No, it's okay, seeing her smile....it's kind of comforting. Um, thanks for deciding to share a room with Ethan for me, I could have just slept on the couch or something" I said managing a smile.

"That's no big deal honestly Ethan was so happy to give up his room, he likes the idea of having a sister and I don't mind sharing with him" he replied. I sat there staring at the rays of light beaming through the sheer purple curtains. I have the opportunity at a new beginning but no idea of where to start. I felt the bed dip and his arm wrap around me, I thought about crying but so many tears have poured out lately that I felt like a dried up river. I turned to look at him, and his eyes gave me peace.

"I don't understand what you're going through none of us do, but Rena we're here for you. I'm here for you, anything you need me to be for you I'll try my best to be that. I wish I could take your pain away, and carry it myself but this is the best I can do. I don't want to lose you Rena, I just want to see you smile and be truly happy" he said looking me right in the eyes.

"I'm not really sure I even know what happiness is anymore" I looked down at my hands, he tilted my chin up so I was looking him directly in the eye.

"And that's okay, because I promise I'll help you find it again" he said squeezing me lightly.

"What would I do without you, my saviour" I joked.

"I don't know but you sure saved me too" he chuckled. There was a knock on the door and it was Vanessa.

"Hey you two, dinner is ready" she smiled at the two of us for a second then went downstairs. Two seconds later Ethan popped in in the doorway smiling.

"C'mon Rena we got to show you what we cooked" he said excitedly, dragging me down the steps. We rounded the corner to the kitchen and there was more food than I was expecting. Spaghetti, steak, casserole, burgers, fries, cookies and even pie.

"Wow guys you cooked all this?" I laughed.

"We didn't know what you'd like so we cooked some basic things" Vanessa spoke up.

"I know that sometimes it seems that I've checked out and I'm not aware of everything you guys do but thank you so much for everything" I stated seriously.

"No need to thank us, you're family" Ms. Vanessa smiled. Family....I always wanted Tara and I to be able to have one of those.

After dinner and a shower I put on a big t-shirt and got ready for bed. I've been out of school for as long as time permitted and it was time for me to go back tomorrow. I stared at the the picture of Tara smiling, she looked so happy even though our home life was much less than ideal. It made me smile a little, I turned off the lights and got into bed hoping for a dreamless night.

I was shaken awake by Ethan's smiling face, I smiled back. He reminds me so much of Tara, that lively spirit and adorable smile.

"Rena it's your first day back, you don't want to be late" he whispered.

"Mmm, course not. You wanna help me pick out an outfit?" I asked. He nodded and walked to my dresser and then to the closet. After brushing my teeth and brushing my hair into a puff, I made my way downstairs in the outfit Ethan had picked out for me. It was a simple blue, long sleeve shirt with a pair of jeans and sneakers. Everyone else was already seated at the table eating breakfast when I joined them.

"Do you like your outfit, I picked the shirt because of Tara" he said eating his pancakes.

"Ethan-" Evan started.

"No it's okay. I love it Ethan, I'm sure she'd be happy that we're remembering her" I replied ruffling his hair. He smiled at me then continued eating, I dug into my own food hopeful for a good day. Vanessa left for work before we were done eating, and when we finally finished we got in the car to head to school. We pulled up to Ethan's school and before getting out he tapped me on the shoulder and said;

"Don't worry Rena, Tara is watching over us she won't let anything bad happen" he said cheerfully. I nodded and smiled at him, then he got out of the car and ran to join his friends. We pulled off and finally our school came into view and I took a deep breath to calm myself.

"It's showtime" I stated.

BLACKBIRD.

Evan held the door open for me as I walked into the school, I was hoping I'd be invisible like usual but that wasn't the case. As I walked to my locker and passed by the other students they would cease all conversation and stare. Evan just gripped my hand tightly and tugged me along.

"Don't worry about them" he whispered in my ear. I nodded and we kept walking until we finally made it to my locker, I put in the combination then opened it "Okay I have to go to class now, but if you need me here's my schedule so you can find me, okay?" he handed me a folded sheet of paper.

"Okay, I'll see you at lunch" I said mustering a smile, he nodded then gave me a quick hug before disappearing down the hall. I gathered my books together then shut my locker only to run straight into Kathy.

"Watch it" she yelled picking up her books the she looked up and realized it was me. "Sorry, blackbir- I mean.....Rena" she said catching herself.

"It's fine" I replied about to turn and take my leave when she grabbed my arm.

"I just wanted to say I'm so sorry about your sister a-and for making your life a living hell. I know this isn't all about me but I feel absolutely terrible and I hope you can find it within your heart to forgive me one day, if you don't that's okay because I wouldn't forgive me either" she blurted out. I was speechless, was she actually apologizing to me? She gave me a smile then walked away. After she was out of sight I exhaled, realizing I had been holding my breath the entire time.

I made my way to class and sat in my usual seat, just waiting for the normal torment from the students and the teachers but it never came. Mr. Vincent even pulled me aside after class offering his condolences for the death of my sister. Class after class it was full of pitiful looks and random people telling me they were sorry for my loss. I felt like a was finally able to breathe after lunch arrived, I picked an empty table and opened 'The Complete Collected Poems of Maya Angelou'. My reading was interrupted by Evan sliding a tray of food in front of me, I looked up at him and cocked my head to the side.

"Eat" he ordered sitting across from me with his own tray.

"Sir, yes sir" I said sarcastically, mimicking a soldier. I bit into my pizza and sighed in content, it was actually pretty good.

"So how'd it go?" he asked.

"How'd what go" I countered, he looked at me then rolled his eyes causing me to laugh a little. "Weird, but that was to be expected. Everyone feels sorry for me though, but I think it's mostly the guilt" I shrugged.

"I figured, at least we have a class together later" he said flashing his signature smile.

"You're right" I agreed.

"Hey I had been wanting to talk to you about what you asked my mom about the other day. That's a big step do you think you're ready for it" he grabbed my hand looking deeply into my eyes. I had asked Ms. Vanessa to let me visit Teresa in prison.

"I think the longer I wait, the more I won't want to go. I need to do this for me, I deserve some closure. I need to just know why" I sighed.

"Of course, I just don't-

"You don't want me to relapse and try to kill myself again" I stated cutting him off. Before he could deny it I spoke again. "I'm as mentally healthy as I'll ever be, I'm here to stay Evan. Don't worry about me" I smiled. I wanted him to believe I was okay even if I didn't believe it.

"Good, I don't know what I'd do without you Rena" he replied holding my hand a little tighter. I can't pin the emotions I feel when he looks at me like this so I do what I always do, brush it off with humor

"You'd die of boredom" I laughed pulling my hand away. I noticed his face fall a little but he quickly shrugged it off and laughed in agreement anyway.

YOU AIN'T GOT NO ONE TO HOLD YOU

I wanted to feel better but I just couldn't get happy, I mean who could if they were in my shoes? Ms.Eden prescribed me so medication for my severe depression and anxiety, my happy pills. When I take them I can't feel anything, no anger, no sadness....nothing. It may surprise people but I'd rather feel pain than be numb like a robot. One downside to not taking the medication is the nightmares. It never fails it's different each time but a nightmare nonetheless.

The one that freaked me out the most was of Tara's funeral, everyone was seated in the pews weeping and I was alone to walk to her casket. When I made it to the front it was her she didn't look how she looked that day she was still beaten and bruised. She was also dressed differently in colorful tights and a matching shirt, it was what she was wearing the day it happened.

The tights were ripped in the crotch area and bloody I wanted to cry but my screams were silent, nothing came out. The people's sobs got louder and louder, I couldn't even think. Just when I felt like I couldn't stand the noise any longer, Tara's eyes opened and she grabbed my arm instantly silencing the cries of the people. She looked directly at me with her cold, lifeless eyes and whispered "Why?"

That was the night Evan told me I should make sure going to visit my mom in prison is what I wanted to do. So after that dream I made my decision, I felt like it was a sign from beyond. Tara wanted me to find out why and I wanted to know too. So as I stood in front of the prison building hesitating to go in I could hear her voice ringing out in my head over and over.

why

why

why

I took a huge deep breath and followed Vanessa inside. We had to sign in and wait for my name to be called, as time went by my palms began to sweat and my heart began to race. In my mind I knew I'd be going in there alone, and I was dreading it but I needed to do this on my own.

"Rena Klein" the guard called. Vanessa gave me a reassuring smile and patted my hand, I stood up and walked through the doors. The guard escort me down a hallway then we stopped at a door and she pat me down. She cleared me and then let me in the room full of other visitors here to see inmates. The guard pointed to a table and there she was, the woman who was supposed to protect and love us unconditionally, Teresa, my mother. She looked horrible but better than her usual crackhead appearance. Which I'm surprised she didn't start using the low grade stuff they deal in here. When I got closer to the table her eyes fell on me and smiled, when I was in arms reach she tried to give me a hug.

"Don't touch me" I said lowly but loud enough for her to hear me. Her smile faltered a little but she regained her composure and started to smile again. I sat down across from her, trying to figure out what to say first.

"You so pretty, healthy I remember when you was born, looking just like your daddy but as you grew up you were the spitting image of me, my mini me. The proudest days of my life is when I had you and Tara" she beamed. It stung to hear her talk about my sister like nothing had ever happened.

"If that was the proudest then I'm sure the worst day of your life is when she was raped and murdered, because I know it was mine" I blurted out. She looked taken aback, I know she wasn't expecting that but I'm not going to sit and converse with her like she's a mother not a monster.

"Rena listen, things aren't just so black and white there is always a grey area-"

"Are you trying to justify letting someone defile and kill your daughter?" I snapped. Before she could say anything else I spoke sternly " Let's not even get started on how you let men rape me and you tried to say I was doing a favor for the family, but fuck that I don't care about me. I just want to know why? Why did you not love us? Why would you let someone hurt her?" I asked, tears forming in my eyes. I sniffled and wiped my face on my sleeve, I saw a single tear fall down her cheek then she shook her head.

"First of all young lady watch ya mouth, I'm still your mama" she scolded.

"Bitch you are not my mother, just because you had the ability to lie on your back and get knocked up with me does not make you my mother. A mother is someone who loves, nurtures, and protects her children. A real mother would die to protect her own from any harm but you, you fed us to the wolves and fucking watched. I was Tara's mother and I had no mother. So now I'm going to ask one more time, why?" I stated. She was silent for a moment but I looked her right in the eye my demeanor never faltering.

"It wasn't my fault, it wasn't supposed to happen. I told him to be gentle and not to hurt her....he took her in my room and locked the door. When I heard her screams I tried to get the door opened I banged and yelled as hard as I could, I tried. I know I'm a sorry excuse of a mother and nothing can ever make up for what I did to you two, and if there is a hell I know that's where I will spend eternity. You have to believe me Rena I loved you two the best way I knew how to, I will never forgive myself for what happened to your sister, or to you for that matter."

"I think I'll sleep a little more peacefully at night knowing you'll never forgive yourself. I hurt every single day Teresa, its like a bottomless pit of pain and even though I know it isn't my fault I feel guilty. To know that one of the people actually at fault feels guilty makes me feel so good, I hope it eats you alive. I hope her screams ring out in your mind when you try to sleep and I hope in every waking moment you see her lifeless face in every single thing you do. I hope the guilt drives you mad until you die and as for him, the other monster. I pray that everything that he did to us someone in prison does to him and when they murder him, I want him choke on his own blood trying to scream for the help that never comes." I let it sink in for a moment and once I realized she had nothing more to say I got up and exited the room.

YOU AIN'T GOT NO ONE TO CARE

I lost myself for a moment there, I lost myself in the anger and the sadness so much that I was drowning and everything I felt spewed out like word vomit. I can't say I regret the things I said to Teresa because I don't but it does scare me. What I felt was so overwhelming that I had to do or say something to get it to stop, and I can assure you I was willing to do anything. I'm not so sure what will happen if I start drowning again.

Evan has been more distant lately, I don't think it's because he is upset with me or anything I think he's just trying to move on from the tragedy. He's made a few new friends they come over every now and then and they're super nice too. They have even invited me to join them a couple times but I don't want to seem like the odd man out, he even got a job to help take some of the weight off of Vanessa. Ethan seems so much happier now, even though he does get sad every now and then he doesn't let it bother him. Vanessa is taking on shifts to support all of us but she loves her job so she doesn't complain.

I feel like I'm stuck in the never ending loop surrounding Tara's death. I can paint on a smile and pretend like I'm fine for everyone else but deep down I know. I wish I was a normal teenager like Evan; making friends, working part time, and stressing about project deadlines. Everyone has started to move on, so why can't I? I know she'd want me to be happy but I can't seem to get there. I walked downstairs to grab me a drink, entering the kitchen I see Evan and a very familiar looking girl, giggling and talking very lowly to each other. When I closed the refrigerator, they jumped finally noticing my presence.

"Hey Rena, there's someone I'd like to meet officially. This is Piper, my girlfriend" he cheesed. Girlfriend? We tell each other everything, so why am I just now finding out about this? Looking at her now I could see she was really pretty. She has piercing green eyes, curly red hair, and beautiful clear skin not a pimple in sight.

"Hi Rena, it's so nice to meet you, I've seen you around school a few times and we have History together" she chirped.

"Oh yeah, I knew you looked familiar. Piper Hobson right?" I asked to which she replied with smile and a nod. "Cool well it was nice to meet you, I'll leave you two to it" I half smiled then left the room before they could object. I can't believe Evan wouldn't tell me about something so important as a girlfriend. How long has this been going on and I didn't even know? I spent the next few days avoiding any kind of interaction with Evan.

I sat on my bed, headphones on, music blasting so loud that I didn't even hear him come in. I finally noticed him when he tapped my foot, which scared me and caused me to kick him off the bed. I snatched my headphones off and jumped up to see if he was okay, when I saw that he was fine we both started laughing.

"My bad, you scared the hell out of me" I laughed. He just shook his head and got up dusting himself off. There was an awkward silence for a minute in between us, I knew this talk was going to happen but I was hoping I could avoid him a whole lot longer.

"Look I'm sorry I didn't tell you about Piper sooner, it's just I got caught up and my mom thought it would be better if I waited"

"What why?" I questioned

"She and Ms. Eden are convinced that you have a crush on me-"

"Wait, what?" I asked bewildered

"Yeah I know, I told her that was crazy to think that" he laughed awkwardly. I just sat there silently, not knowing what to say next. I don't see him in that way, do I? I just know that whatever this is I feel is going to cause problems, I'm not even sure what this feeling is. If I say nothing I know he's going to drift further away so I did what was best.

"There is no way that I could like you like that" I laughed in agreement.

IF YOU'D ONLY UNDERSTAND, DEAR

Our deep conversations became fewer until they were basically nonexistent, I miss Evan. I know I see him everyday but I mean he's changing....without me. I'm falling behind, and I can't keep up with everyone else while they're healing. Though I still feel like I'm wallowing in the festering wound that is the grief I can't get rid of.

"Rena" Ms. Eden said snapping me out of my daze.

"Yes" I replied.

"I asked you how have things been" she reiterated.

"Fine, things have been getting along well. Ethan is doing so much better in school, Vanessa is the best support system I could ever have, and Evan and I are closer than ever" I said plastering the most superficial smile on my face I could muster.

"That's amazing, I'm happy to hear that. Have you made any new friends?" she piqued.

"Not a friend yet, per se but there is this this girl from my Theater class that invited me out to the movies with a couple of other people" I said lying straight through my teeth.

"Rena that is wonderful, you know I'm so proud of you and everything you are becoming and I know Tara would be proud of you too. You are in what we call recovery, the pain of a tragedy like this never really goes away but you are beginning to learn how to cope with it so it doesn't effect your everyday life" she smiled at me, and I felt bad because none of what I said is true. I lied because I feel like I'm drowning again. It's been 8 months and it feels like it just happened yesterday. I don't sleep that much anymore because all I get is nightmare after nightmare.

After my session with Ms. Eden I stood outside waiting for Vanessa to pick me up and instead Evan pulled up with Piper in the passenger seat. I got in the car very confused at why he was picking me up and very annoyed at the fact that his girlfriend was with him.

"Mom is pulling an extra shift so she told me to come pick you up" he stated. I just nodded and put my earbuds in, when things get overwhelming, I do whatever it takes to block it out. We pulled up to an unfamiliar house, I'm guessing to drop Piper off because after awkwardly long makeout she finally got out. Evan turned around and tapped my leg, I took one of my earbuds out to see what he was bothering me for. "Woah, don't bite my head off, I just wanted to let you know you could get in the front now" he laughed.

"No thanks" I replied, and returned to my solitude of music. I could feel him looking at me for a few more seconds then he finally turned back around and started the car. When we got home I stormed into the house, and closed the door in his face. In my defense I did not know he was that close behind me I thought it would take him a few minutes to get out of the car. He caught me right in front of my room by grabbing my hand. I ripped my earbuds out, now officially pissed off. "What" I snatched my hand away from him.

"What the hell is wrong with you, you've been acting so distant and annoyed" he replied.

"I just had a bad day" I shrugged.

"No I mean for the last few months, you've been acting like I ran over your puppy. I've been meaning to talk to you about it but I've just been so busy with-"

"With Piper, right?" I cut him off, rolling my eyes.

"Not just Piper, I have a life, unlike you" he replied and I saw the moment he realized what he said because I could see the remorse in his eyes. "Shit, Rena I did not mean that-"

"Get the fuck away from me Evan. You meant what you said and I know you did because if you didn't it would have never crossed your mind to say it" replied fighting back tears. I entered my room, slamming the door and locking it behind me. I cried into my pillow because I was hurt, and it hurt so much because it was true. I don't know how to fix what's wrong with me, and no one can help me; not Ms. Eden, not Vanessa, not even Evan.

NOBODY WANTS YOU ANYWHERE

My days started to blur together, days without having anyone to talk to, and sleepless nights. The same week of the argument I'd wake up from my few hours of sleep to notes slid under my door from Evan. I'm sure he was apologizing some more but I never opened a single one and after a while the notes stopped coming.

It really didn't matter anymore anyway, because as time went on the more numb I got. I think I'm slowly but surely losing my mind, and I have no solace. So when my birthday rolled around, I was not in a celebratory mood. I came out of my room and walked into the kitchen to find a single cupcake sitting on the counter and a card beside it. It read:

Happy Birthday Rena, I know you've been really sad so I hope this cheers you up. Tara told me your birthday and I made sure to never forget, so mom and I waited till you went to sleep to make this for you. I hope you have a good day, love you - Ethan

Dear Rena, I'm so proud of the woman you've become despite all of the weight on your shoulders. Ever since I was a little girl I had always wanted a daughter, and my dream didn't come true until I met you. Have a magical birthday, and check the garage for a surprise -Vanessa

I smiled and I felt that maybe today wouldn't be so bad. I went to the garage and there was a car with a bow on it. Not one of those expensive ass cars you read about teenagers getting in books but it was a 2006 Ford Fusion. Don't get me wrong I was grateful for my gift, it was the first time in a long time that I had gotten anything for my birthday. Though I couldn't help but notice that Evan didn't write anything on the card or even send me a text. I ate my cupcake and got dressed for school and actually styled my hair for once.

When I made it to school, everything went how it normally does. It was boring and lonely, at lunch I walked past Evan and he looked at me and said nothing. Maybe it was time for me to stop being so stubborn, so I walked up to him and his group of friends at their table.

"Hey" I said and they all went silent, I think they were just as surprised as he was.

"You lost" he asked.

"Huh?" I questioned confused at his attitude.

"Are you lost?" he said a little more slowly causing one of his friends to snicker.

"Oh...um, no I was just wondering if you forgot what today was"

"What Taco Tuesday?" he replied. I could tell by his body language that he was mad at me, but did he really forget?

"No...my birthday" I said

"Ok" he answered nonchalantly. I don't know if he was just putting on a show for everyone else or if he was really didn't care but either way I couldn't tell the difference. I had nothing more to say so I just walked away then heard someone say to him.

"I think you hurt her feelings" and shortly after I heard him say "I don't care."

I decided to cut my day short and just go home. I pulled up I saw Vanessa was home, so I won't be able to go without questioning. When I walked inside she already had her scrubs on ready to go to work.

"Rena, what are you doing home" she questioned. I sat on the stool and just dropped my head.

"It's just one of those days" I sighed.

"I'm sure it'll get better sweetie, I planned on taking us all out on a family outing tonight but they called me in to work, so we'll go to tomorrow night" she replied hugging me tightly.

"That's fine, I'm gonna go lie down now" I said quietly. I was so tired, too tired to deal with these emotions. So I laid on my bed and drifted off to sleep. In my dream there was this big beautiful house in the middle of nowhere and when I went inside and Tara was sitting on the floor playing with a doll house.

"Rena, come play with me" she smiled. This wasn't like every other nightmare I had, Tara wasn't dead this version of her was literally identical to how she was when she was alive. She was happy, without a care in the world. I sat down next to her my eyes starting to tear up. "What's wrong?" she asked touching my cheek.

"It's just, I miss you" I answered, tears falling now.

"I'm okay Rena, stop worrying. You need to be happy now" she said.

"I can't seem to get happy" I choked out.

"I know, and whenever stuff gets too hard, just remember I'll always be waiting here for you" she smiled her contagious smile again. Then I sat straight up in bed, and started to cry, that was not a nightmare. It felt like the sign that I needed, I actually have a chance to be happy again. I checked my phone and it was a few minutes after school ended and still nothing from Evan. I went into the bathroom and looked at myself in the mirror. I looked so tired, bags under my eyes, messy hair, chapped lips. Nothing has changed since my life collapsed before my eyes and nothing will change. I was drowning again but only I know how to save myself from it.

I turned on the hot water and put the stopper in for a bath as it ran I went to the kitchen, grabbed what I needed then went back into the bathroom. It was halfway full now and I sat down in it which caused the water to rise a little more. I sighed, I never thought that I'd resort to this but I have nothing else left to stay for. Tara was my reason but she's not here anymore and Vanessa, Evan, and Ethan all have each other so they'll get through this.

The running of the water was kind of soothing in the moment. I sighed and took the knife and cut a vertical line from my wrist up. I winced at the pain, it hurt so bad, my tears started to blur my vision but it did not stop me from repeating it on my other arm. The pain will be over soon I thought as I closed my eyes and all I could see was Tara smiling at me finally, I am a caged bird no more.